D1708088

TALES OF HEAVEN AND EARTH

Christian Rudel has been exploring
South America for thirty years. He writes
for various magazines and is the author
of several books about Mexico and the history
of the indigenous peoples of South America.

Cover design by Peter Bennett

Published by Creative Education
123 South Broad Street, Mankato, Minnesota 56001
Creative Education is an imprint
of The Creative Company

Library of Congress Cataloging-in-Publication Data

Rudel, Christian.
[Enfants de a luné. English]
Children of the moon / by Christian Rudel;
illustrated by Etienne Souppart;
translated by Simona Sideri.
p. cm. — (Tales of heaven and earth)
Summary: In this Yanomami tale, a youngster searches for the
truth of the Moon Spirit. Explanatory sidebars present information
about the Yanomami way of life.
ISBN 0-88682-829-5

1. Yanomami Indians—Folklore. 2. Yanomami mythology.
3. Tales—Amazon River Region. [1. Yanomami Indians—Folklore.
2. Indians of South America—Folklore. 3. Folklore—Amazon River Region.]
I. Souppart, Etienne, ill. II. Title. III. Series.
F2520.1.Y3R8313   1997
398.2'08998—dc20   96-34799

6 5 4 3 2 1

CHILDREN
OF
THE
MOON

BY CHRISTIAN RUDEL

ILLUSTRATED BY ETIENNE SOUPPART

TRANSLATED BY SIMONA SIDERI

☕ CREATIVE EDUCATION

Yanomami hunters return laden with prey for a feast.

The curassow, a bird of the rainforest, is awkward in flight. It can often be seen searching for fruit on the forest floor.

The Yanomami live in large groups made up of several different families. The building they live in is called a *shabono*.

VENEZUELA

AMAZON BASIN

BRAZIL

South America

The Yanomami live in southern Venezuela, near the source of the Orinoco River, and across the border in Brazil.

The hunting had been good and the small group of Yanomami hunters returned home weighed down with prey. They had caught some spider monkeys, a tapir, and several curassow, which they put down in the middle of the *shabono*. The carcasses were quickly cleaned and the meat was cut into pieces and cooked. The feast which followed went on all through the night, beneath the watchful stare of a huge full moon.

While the hunters were away, the other men had stayed behind to protect the women and children. Every

The circular *shabono* is about 55 yards (50 m) in diameter and can hold up to 100 people. The roof is made of thick leaves that almost reach the ground on the outside. In the middle is a clearing which is open to the sky, and round like the moon—an important symbol for the Yanomami. This is where tribespeople hold meetings. Around the central clearing runs a covered corridor where families sleep and cook.

night they had sung and danced, calling on the Moon spirit to bring the hunters luck. Tonight, instead of the usual, dull plantain stew, they had their reward—an extra-large ration of meat.

After they had finished eating, the men carried on talking around the blazing fire. The hunters remembered how they had left the *shabono* in silence, treading paths that they alone knew. At the slightest noise they all stopped, frozen in their tracks. On the way home they had seen a dying monkey. It would have been a bad omen, if they had seen it at the start of the hunt.

Bored with these stories, the children went back to their own games. They played at being hunters: spying out their prey high up in the branches, they pulled back their bow strings to send silent arrows flying through the air. Tired of this game, the boys paired off for a wrestling competition. For this, the Yanomami have a strict set of rules, which to us would seem more like an endurance test than a fight. One person stands still, with his arms hanging at his sides, while his opponent beats him with a heavy stick. The person receiving the beating is not allowed to defend himself in any way: he must not move or cry out or even flinch.

Each family has its own space in the corridor. The family's hammocks hang from the roof beams around their cooking fire. Wood is stacked toward the back, where the roof is lowest.

After the meal, the children play among themselves and fight.

Kiyéko and his friends are play-fighting. For many of the peoples of America, Africa, and Asia, such competitions are a way of building strength. Each tribe or group has its own rules. Fights may also be part of tribal initiation—tests and trials young people must undergo before they are known as adults.

The forest and its many waterways provide plenty of food. The Yanomami eat fish, birds, snakes, and caymans, as well as insects such as termites and their larvae.

After a set number of blows, the two players change places.

Tonight Kiyéko was up against Moriwé, a big, burly boy a few years older than him and soon to become a hunter. The blows fell thick and fast on Kiyéko's shoulders and on his head and chest. He couldn't stand it any more, and hiding his face in his hands, he tried to move out of the way. Moriwé carried on beating him until Kiyéko cried out in pain. From the group of adults around the empty pot, a voice thundered out: "Kiyéko, stand up straight. Act like the true child of the Moon that you are. And when your turn comes, hit back as hard as you can."

Bracing himself to receive more blows, and sniffing back his tears, Kiyéko took up his place once again.

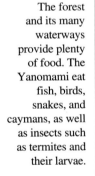

Kiyéko proves that he too is a son of the Moon.

Blood was trickling down his face, but there was no time to wipe it off. At last, it was his turn to hit Moriwé, but although he called on all his strength, the older boy seemed hardly to feel the blows. "I am a child of the Moon, a true child of the Moon," Kiyéko repeated to himself, clenching the stick tightly in his small hands.

He had heard the story many times and knew it well. Nevertheless, when the fighting was over and the other children had run off to chase a dog, he approached his father. "Tell me about the children of the Moon?" he asked. But Hébéwé, his father, did not hear him, or perhaps he just chose not to answer. He had told the story many times and had no wish to start again. Not far from him sat Horonami. The old shaman had finished his prayers of thanks to the spirits for bringing the hunters luck and providing plentiful game. "Kiyéko," he called the boy, "I will tell you."

Kiyéko was afraid of the old man. He always spoke so loudly. Sometimes, when all was quiet in the *shabono,* he would suddenly start running around in a frenzy. But now the boy's curiosity overcame his fear.

"A long time ago," the shaman began,

The Yanomami's world is full of spirits who represent all the forces of the universe and every living thing within it. For example, there is a spirit of the Milky Way, a spirit of the Whirlwind, a spirit of Darkness, a Jaguar spirit, a Vulture spirit, a Toad spirit . . .

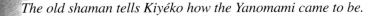

The old shaman tells Kiyéko how the Yanomami came to be.

"in the whole forest, there lived only one man, his wife, and their child. They lived like we do, except that they were utterly alone. They collected plantains and hunted for meat, and when they were ill, the man healed them using his knowledge of plants.

"One day, the man died. His wife and son collected wood and made a bonfire to burn the body, just as we do today. When night fell, the fire went out and the ashes cooled. All of a sudden, the son noticed a dark shadow crouching over the embers and he heard a crunching sound. Trying to hide his fear, he approached the fire. The shadow moved and he recognized Moon, feeding on his father's bones.

"Remember, Kiyéko, that in those days, when the world was young, Moon didn't live up in the sky. He was a spirit who had lived inside the man until that very moment. The boy cried out, but Moon just carried on feeding. Hearing his shout, the boy's mother rushed outside in a fury. 'Quick!' she cried, 'Go and get your bow and arrow!'

"Her son ran off to fetch his weapons, but already Moon was fleeing. By the time the boy had returned and drawn his bow, Moon was no more than a shining light

Spirits may become visible to shamans, who travel to their world and speak to them. Some shamans turn into spirits to use their power and knowledge. Many spirits are ancestors of the Yanomami, such as the Moon spirit in this story.

The Yanomami believe in other spirits—*hékuras*—which are closer to the human world. They live in animals and natural phenomena, and accompany shamans on journeys. A shaman calls on spirits to cure diseases and bring success to hunters. He protects his community from spirits sent by enemy shamans or sends his own against his tribe's enemies.

They grew from drops of blood shed by the Moon.

high up among the stars. He took aim and a long, thin arrow sped through the sky and hit Moon. It was only a tiny cut, but Moon began to bleed. As each drop of blood fell to earth, it turned into a Yanomami. Soon there were hundreds of us and we spread across the earth. That is why we are all children of the Moon. Born from blood, we are strong and fearless warriors. Do you understand my little Kiyéko?" asked Horonami, the old shaman, at last.

"Yes," answered the boy. He looked up through the trees behind which the moon was disappearing and added, "I want to grow up to be strong, like every Yanomami should be."

The children spy on Horonami in the forest.

The Yanomami hang their hunting trophies (animal heads, feathers, fish bones) from the roof around their fireplace. These are proof of the hunter's skill and also serve as offerings to the spirits, to ask their blessing for future hunts.

A few days passed and the gang of children were going to spend the day hunting in the forest. Moriwé-the-Mighty picked up some arrows and his bow, which was a smaller copy of the one used by the hunters. Followed by his friends, he set off along the path through the vegetable garden. Here, pumpkins grew under the banana trees while beyond stretched the vast, dark forest.

"Silence," barked Moriwé, leading the way.

Not even the birds noticed the children passing, for they walked through the trees as silently as hunters.

As soon as he can stand, a boy is given a small copy of the bow his father carries. The Yanomami are quite short (about 5.2 feet or 1.6 meters on average) but their bows are over 6.5 feet or 2 meters high and make the hunters feel invincible. The bows are hand-crafted from palm wood: the complicated work takes many hours.

The shaman seems to be talking to a liana!

The arrowheads are made from palm wood with a number of horizontal cuts across them. When they hit their target, they shatter inside the animal's flesh, allowing the poison they have been dipped in to spread more quickly through the bloodstream.

The Yanomami grow beans, tomatoes, and pumpkins, as well as tobacco and sometimes cotton. The forest soil is poor and there are no fertilizers to enrich it. After five or six years all the nutrients in the soil are used up and nothing will grow, so the tribespeople move their garden to a new patch of land.

Suddenly, they all stopped short: there was somebody there, his back toward them, just an arrow's flight away. It was Horonami, the shaman. Disappointed, the children turned back—all except for Kiyéko who, since the other evening, felt that Horonami was his special friend.

He continued to watch the shaman, who remained standing quite still. Every now and then, Horonami would mutter to himself, but Kiyéko couldn't hear what he was saying. Finally, the shaman grasped a large liana, cut it, and moved on, searching for something. He cut another smaller liana and turned to head back toward the *shabono*. He noticed Kiyéko, but didn't seem at all surprised to find him standing there.

"Are you out hunting, Kiyéko?" the shaman asked in a friendly voice. "I've been cutting lianas to make curare poison for the big hunt tomorrow," he explained.

Encouraged by his smile, Kiyéko asked, "Who were you speaking to? I couldn't see anyone with you."

Horonami smiled again. "When you uproot a plant, or cut down a tree, or indeed kill any living being, you must

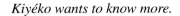

ask its spirit for permission. And you must tell the plant or tree what you are going to do. That liana I cut down earlier was probably asking itself why, out of all the lianas in the forest, I had picked that very one. I was explaining that it was the best one I could find, being thick and strong. I told it I would use it to make good curare which would provide us with a plentiful catch. Do you understand now?"

The old shaman didn't give Kiyéko time to answer. He obviously felt like talking today. "Do you know how curare saved our lives, the lives of all the Yanomami people?" He didn't wait for an answer. "Long, long ago there was a man-eating jaguar in the jungle. No one was able to kill it and every day it ate one or two more people. Soon there would be nobody left. That is when the spirit of the curare plant took the shape of a man. His name was Mamokoriyoma and his skin was so leathery and tasted so bitter that the jaguar didn't want to eat him. One day Mamokoriyoma saved a young woman from the jaws of the jaguar. She climbed to safety onto the *shabono* roof. This same woman later had children, the twins Yoawe and Omawe, who grew up to be brilliant

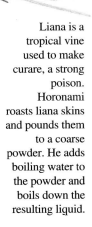

Liana is a tropical vine used to make curare, a strong poison. Horonami roasts liana skins and pounds them to a coarse powder. He adds boiling water to the powder and boils down the resulting liquid.

Only the shaman can prepare the curare poison because only he has learned the secret recipe. He must follow certain rules that only he knows. And he must fast before cutting the lianas and must work in complete silence.

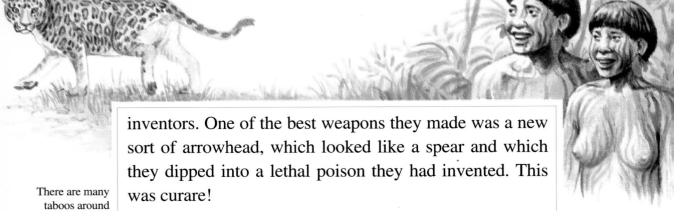

inventors. One of the best weapons they made was a new sort of arrowhead, which looked like a spear and which they dipped into a lethal poison they had invented. This was curare!

"The last hunters still remaining alive used the twins' poisoned arrows to kill the man-eating jaguar, so we had peace once again. Without curare we would all have been long dead!"

Kiyéko and the old man walked on in silence. It had rained the night before and the path was muddy. Suddenly Kiyéko spotted a toad, almost hidden beneath a tangle of roots. He had already raised his bow when Horonami stopped him.

"Don't hurt the toad. He may have been a great warrior once." Then, after a few moments' hesitation he added, "Here, if you wrap this strip of bark around your waist you can come with me and watch me prepare the poison."

There are many taboos around the preparation of curare. It is said that if children see the poison being prepared, they will get very bad stomachaches. To avoid this, they can wear a wide strip of bark wrapped around their waist.

Most indigenous peoples of South America believe that every living thing has a spirit that never dies. When a man dies, for example, his spirit may go and live in a blade of grass. The Plains Indians of North America believe the spirits of their ancestors dwell in the whispering wind and the fluttering leaves.

The next morning, Moriwé's little sister is ill.

The *shabono* was all in a flutter the next morning. Hayéma, Moriwé's younger sister, was ill. She lay listlessly in her hammock, staring at the roof and refusing to eat her breakfast of plantain broth. Nor would she sip any honeyed water. Moriwé had spread the word among his friends and soon the children were gathered around Hayéma's hammock, trying to cheer her up. But she wouldn't even smile.

Her mother, Ratimi, guessed the reason for her illness straightaway. "An enemy shaman has cast a spell over

Like almost all other Amazonian peoples, the Yanomami believe that every human being has a double in the animal world to which they are closely tied. A child's double may be a small blue lizard; a woman's double is often an otter.

us," she said. "Remember those people who visited us last month? Maybe their shaman has done this. They are jealous because our men are better hunters than theirs. But why my little Hayéma?"

Ratimi's sister went to find Horonami. But the shaman had gotten up early that day to search the forest for the herbs and seeds he used to make hallucinogenic powder. When he got back he went straight to the sickbed.

One glance at Hayéma told him the problem. "She has lost her image, her double. We must find it quickly." Picking up some palm leaves, he carefully began to sweep the ground under the family's hammocks, around the fire, and in the wood store. There was nothing. Then he turned toward the children, "We will have to sweep the path and all the places where Hayéma ran and played yesterday. I need your help!"

They all set to work, but they found nothing along the forest paths. At this point, Horonami realized he was dealing with a powerful enemy shaman and returned to the *shabono* where Hayéma still lay staring blankly. It was time that Horonami consulted his *hékuras*.

He asked Turawé, Hayéma's

A hallucinogen is a substance that alters our perception of reality and may produce dreams and visions. The Amazonian peoples know of many hallucinogenic plants.

Hékuras are spirits.

16

It must be found quickly.

Each tribe has its own methods for making hallucinogenic powders and potions. The process is generally complicated and the person preparing the drug must have fasted for a long time, as must anyone who takes it.

father, to blow hallucino-genic powder into his nostrils. The effect was instant: the shaman closed his eyes and sweat began pouring down his forehead, dripping off the tip of his nose. At first he held still, then he began to move, dancing faster and faster, making shrill cries while whirling around the sick girl. He mimed a fierce fight, lashing out at an invisible enemy with a broken bow he had found in the wood pile. He fell, got up, hit out again, held his head writhing in pain and then jumped up to fight again. Ratimi and her neighbors watched in silence. The afternoon passed in this way until at last, exhausted, Horonami stopped. He managed to find the strength to go to his hearth, returning with a packet of dried herbs. He selected some leaves and asked for boiling water with which to make an infusion. Hayéma drank it and immediately fell asleep.

Yanomami make hallucinogens from bark or sap of the *Virola,* a tree with yellow flowers that give out a bitter smell.

17

"She's much better," declared Horonami. "I found her double and brought it back. The shaman from the *shabono* down the river had taken it. He tried to race off with it, through the forest and up toward the sun. He had gathered his *hékuras* around him for protection and it was they who beat me and scratched me. The battle was fierce and it was very hot up there, but I won."

His face shone with sweat, but he was happy. When Hayéma woke up a little later, she smiled and jumped out of her hammock. There was not a trace of the illness. Everyone cheered Horonami. He had saved the day!

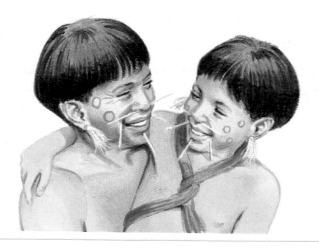

Shimiwé dies, killed by an enemy warrior.

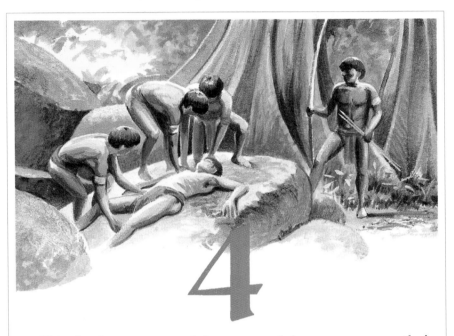

Fights often break out between the inhabitants of different *shabonos*. The Yanomami blame everything, from an accident to a bad hunt or the loss of possessions, on evil spirits. They believe these have been sent against them by shamans from other tribes.

Shimiwé was a good hunter and knew every path in the forest. He was also a great fighter whose arrows had struck down dozens of enemies. But now, on his way home from a hunting expedition, he had been wounded by an enemy warrior. He was lagging behind his companions, so no one saw him fall. Despite his terrible wounds, he somehow managed to reach the *shabono*. His body was found in the undergrowth, just a few steps from the entrance, lying curled up, but still holding his bow tightly.

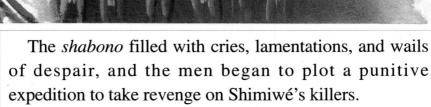

The Yanomami believe that when someone dies, it is because an evil spirit has been sent against them by an enemy. Thus every death must be avenged. After consulting with his *hékuras,* the shaman decides which day is best for the task, and whether the warriors should lay a simple ambush to kill an enemy warrior, or instead capture a woman. Any bad omen, like a dead animal on their path, will cause the mission to fail.

The *shabono* filled with cries, lamentations, and wails of despair, and the men began to plot a punitive expedition to take revenge on Shimiwé's killers.

When the wood for the funeral pyre was stacked up high, the people gathered around and the shaman began to speak. He gestured in the air, danced, and shrieked loudly, listing Shimiwé's many qualities and innumerable exploits to the *hékuras.* The fire burst into flame and soon a tall column of thick black smoke was rising above the tree tops, stretching up to the moon.

The next day, as soon as he got up, Yétirawé, the dead man's brother, went to examine the pile of ashes and bits of blackened wood that were all that remained of the pyre. He crouched down with his left hand behind his back, using his right hand to search among the warm cinders for any bones that might be left. He put the few pieces he found in a gourd and then, using a pestle, smashed them to a fine grey powder. He poured this into another container and sealed it. The final funeral would take place a week later.

Kiyéko had often seen funeral pyres burn, but he had never asked himself why this was done. It had so far been to him just a meaningless tradition. Now he wanted

All the Yanomami people burn their dead. Some do so right after the death, whereas in other tribes the body is exposed in the forest, out of reach of meat-eating animals, and left to decompose before the skeleton is burnt.

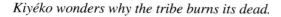
Kiyéko wonders why the tribe burns its dead.

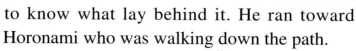

to know what lay behind it. He ran toward Horonami who was walking down the path.

"Why do we burn the dead?" he asked breathlessly. Horonami looked at the boy, nodded, and half-smiled. Finally he answered: "The flames and the smoke carry the spirits of the dead high up to the sky where the thunder dwells."

This wasn't enough for Kiyéko, and by now the other children had gathered around the shaman to hear his words. He continued the story: "Long, long ago, an old woman called Préyoma laid this curse on us after one of our ancestors had stolen fire from the first man who had any. This is what happened. When time began, the Yanomami had no fire. We ate our food cold and raw. For example, pieces of meat were just washed and beaten between two stones to get all the blood out. Then they were ready to eat.

"But there was one man among us who possessed fire. His name was Iwariwé, but he was so mean, he refused to share it with the rest of us. He kept his fire hidden under his tongue so that no one could steal it. So, when the rains came, and the cold, when everyone was shivering

The family drinks a plantain soup specially prepared with some of the powder added to it. This is believed to stop the spirit of the dead from wandering in the forest and meeting with evil spirits. The same ritual is performed after the death of a faithful dog that has been a good hunter.

The remains of the burnt bones are carefully pounded into a powder and used some weeks later in another ritual. This marks the final farewell to the dead person, whose name must never be mentioned again.

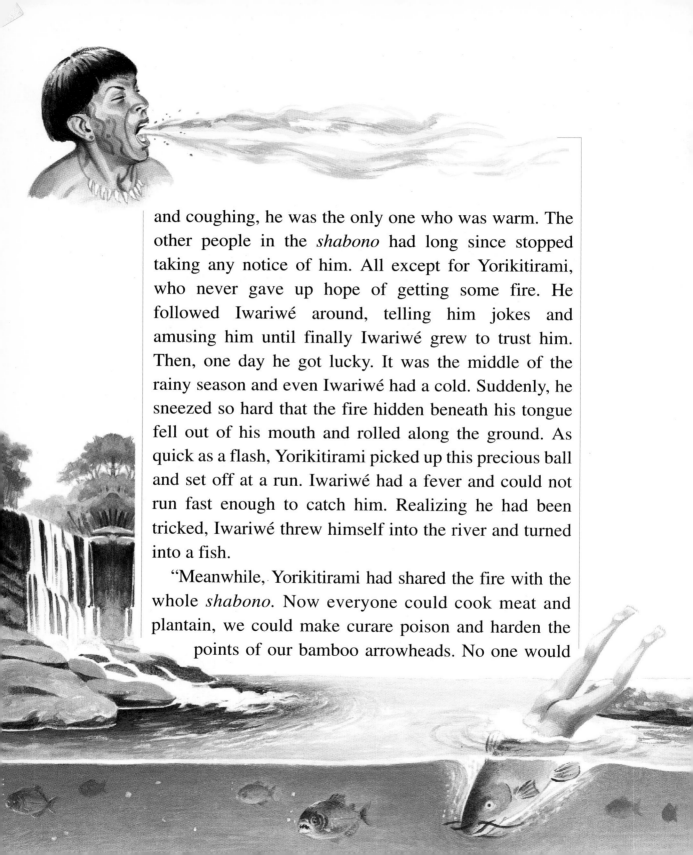

and coughing, he was the only one who was warm. The other people in the *shabono* had long since stopped taking any notice of him. All except for Yorikitirami, who never gave up hope of getting some fire. He followed Iwariwé around, telling him jokes and amusing him until finally Iwariwé grew to trust him. Then, one day he got lucky. It was the middle of the rainy season and even Iwariwé had a cold. Suddenly, he sneezed so hard that the fire hidden beneath his tongue fell out of his mouth and rolled along the ground. As quick as a flash, Yorikitirami picked up this precious ball and set off at a run. Iwariwé had a fever and could not run fast enough to catch him. Realizing he had been tricked, Iwariwé threw himself into the river and turned into a fish.

"Meanwhile, Yorikitirami had shared the fire with the whole *shabono*. Now everyone could cook meat and plantain, we could make curare poison and harden the points of our bamboo arrowheads. No one would

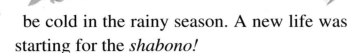

be cold in the rainy season. A new life was starting for the *shabono!*

"Yorikitirami jumped for joy. He jumped so high that he got stuck up a tree, and when he tried to get down he found he had turned into a bird, a black bird with a huge red and yellow beak, the color of fire. He had become a toucan!

A toucan is a medium-sized climbing bird that lives in the tropical forest. It is easily recognized by its enormous, but light and fragile, beak. Its feathers are mainly black on its body, with flames of loud color splashed over the neck and chest. Yanomami men use toucan feathers as decorative armbands.

"The women were already busying themselves cooking the first hot meal, so only a few of the men saw Yorikitirami's transformation. But everyone heard Préyoma when she rushed into the center of the *shabono* shouting, 'This fire will make you suffer. You should have left it with he who guarded it. It was his personal power, his secret. You would have been happier without it.' As she rushed off she screamed a final warning: 'You and all your descendants after you will burn in fire!' And then she turned into a tiny orange insect, the sort that I call on to cure a fever.

"From that day on, after we die, we must pass through fire so that our spirit can rest easy and no evil spirit will force us to wander restlessly in the forest. This is why we burn our dead, young Kiyéko."

Kiyéko was proud that Horonami's explanation had been meant for him. He was glad that the other children realized the old shaman was his friend. Even Moriwé, the leader of the gang, had noticed and seemed to treat him with more respect.

Kiyéko hears a mysterious name mentioned.

The *shabono* had been in a high state of excitement till late into the night. There had been another feast, as once again the hunters had returned with an enormous catch. The women had prepared the meat and roasted the plantains. Everyone had eaten their fill.

And that's when it had happened. One of the hunters had begun to speak, getting more and more angry and violent. He accused another hunter of having stolen his arrowheads and of having put a curse on him to stop him from ever catching any game.

"Puriwariwé is evil. He must die. He will die soon!" he shouted.

Silence fell on the *shabono*. The blue light of the moon filtered through the huge trees as the fires slowly went out. But the terrible cry still echoed through the night, "Puriwariwé will die soon!"

Kiyéko turned to his father to ask who Puriwariwé was, but Hébéwé made vigorous signs for him to be quiet. Later Kiyéko asked his young friends. No answer. So the next day, when he saw Horonami walking along the river, he left his playmates and ran toward him.

"Last night one of the hunters was angry with Puri . . ."

But he wasn't allowed to finish. With an authoritative gesture of his stick, Horonami ordered the boy to be silent. Then he explained.

"That name you heard was Ayawé's secret name, his real name. You see, everyone has a secret name."

"Me too?"

"Yes, of course you do. I gave it to you myself the day

It is only when a person's secret name is given to him that he becomes a true member of the community.

Horonami explains the powers of secret names.

you were born, as I carried you around the *shabono.* Soon I will tell you what it is. But remember, you must never say anyone's secret name out loud. If an enemy hunter heard you, or an evil spirit, they might easily use it to hurt that person. They could make him ill, steal his double, or even kill him. Only I would be able to protect him. I would need to gather my *hékuras* around me to fight off the illness. Or I might have to set off on a long journey far away to seek his lost soul. It would take days and days, and at the end of my journey I might have to fight to get it back."

"But you could?"

"Yes," answered Horonami slowly, "but I am getting old now; soon I will die."

"When I am grown up I could take your place," Kiyéko cried excitedly. "I could protect the *shabono* against bad spirits. I could collect lianas like you do and turn them into poisonous snakes which I would leave on our enemies' path. . . ."

Horonami stopped in the middle of the

The power of a secret name is thought to be enormous. So, for example, to name a dead person is to call up his ghost. There are lots of rules about using people's secret names. To avoid any unfortunate mistakes, children are not told their parents' secret names.

When hunting, the Yanomami mustn't name their prey or even point it out, in case it should disappear or not show itself at all. To name something you want is to ensure you won't get it! There are many words and phrases that can be used to identify an animal easily and without risk.

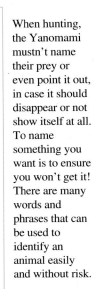

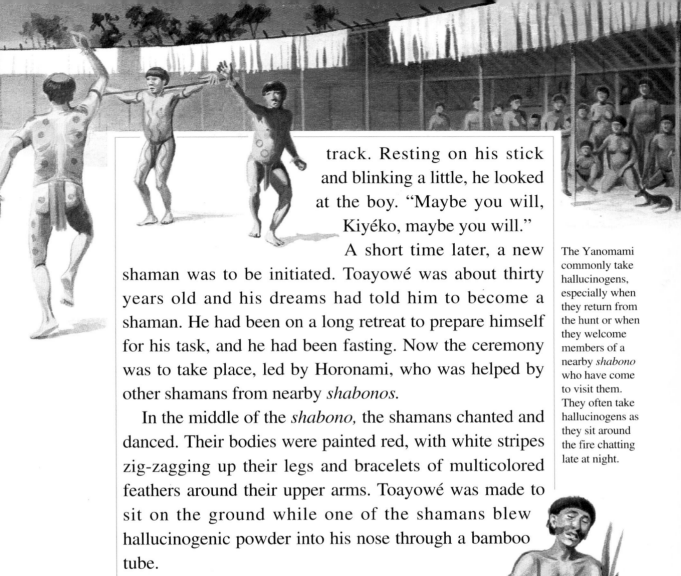

track. Resting on his stick and blinking a little, he looked at the boy. "Maybe you will, Kiyéko, maybe you will."

A short time later, a new shaman was to be initiated. Toayowé was about thirty years old and his dreams had told him to become a shaman. He had been on a long retreat to prepare himself for his task, and he had been fasting. Now the ceremony was to take place, led by Horonami, who was helped by other shamans from nearby *shabonos*.

In the middle of the *shabono,* the shamans chanted and danced. Their bodies were painted red, with white stripes zig-zagging up their legs and bracelets of multicolored feathers around their upper arms. Toayowé was made to sit on the ground while one of the shamans blew hallucinogenic powder into his nose through a bamboo tube.

Soon the drug took effect. Toayowé's eyes rolled back in his head, showing the whites, and he took on a dazed expression. Sweat began to pour down his cheeks and he was violently sick. The other shamans

The Yanomami commonly take hallucinogens, especially when they return from the hunt or when they welcome members of a nearby *shabono* who have come to visit them. They often take hallucinogens as they sit around the fire chatting late at night.

It takes a long time to initiate a shaman.

The Yanomami believe that the colorful visions produced by the hallucinogens are actually the real world, the world where spirits live. So, they want to visit it often by taking the drug. But only the shamans can actually speak to the spirits.

danced around him, calling on the *hékuras,* asking them to leave their homes on the other side of the river or in the rocks, to come and take possession of Toayowé. But the *hékuras* wouldn't answer and the shamans had to dance and plead with them for a long time. At last a rustling of leaves was heard: the *hékuras* had arrived.

"Can you see the Vulture spirit?" asked Horonami.

"Yes, I see it," answered Toayowé.

"Can you see the Moon spirit?"

"Yes, I see it. It is entering into me."

Questions and answers followed each other. From time to time, Toayowé was given more of the hallucinogen. All night the ceremony went on while, one by one, the people crept quietly to their beds.

The ritual ran its course, night after night. Always under the influence of drugs, the pupil shaman answered his teachers' questions. He described his dreams and

But Kiyéko's mind is made up: he too will be a shaman.

"I rise up in the sky, toward the sun. Come with me, follow my visions. Follow me beyond the tallest tree tops. Look at these birds and butterflies. You will never see such colors on earth. I rise up in the sky, toward the sun."
Shaman's chant.

visions and repeated the lessons that he had been taught, the invocations and sacred chants he would need in order to call the *hékuras* and protect his people. But as time went by he became weaker and weaker.

After seven days and seven nights, the trial ended. Kiyéko, who had tried to stay awake to follow the ritual, had hardly understood any of it. But a few days later, when Horonami asked him if he still wanted to become a shaman, he answered "Yes" without any hesitation.

"And I will be a hunter and a warrior," declared Moriwé, who was walking beside them, brandishing his bow. "That is good," thought Horonami, looking fondly at the two boys, "the *shabono* will prosper."

The Yanomami community living in a *shabono* is made up of various extended families who have gathered together. Each family consists of a couple with their children and grand-children, as well as a number of other close blood-relatives. The community grows through marriage, and the larger it is, the more powerful is its chief.

THE AMAZON BASIN

Rubber is made from latex, the sap of the rubber tree.

Rubber bark is cut so that the latex can drip into the cup hung on the tree.

The Yanomami originally lived near the source of the Orinoco River beneath Mount Sierra Parima.

Piranhas are fierce meat-eating fish. The people of the Amazon use their sharp teeth as razors or arrowheads.

The Amazon River and its tributaries flow through the Amazon basin. This area of some 2.5 million square miles (7 million sq km) (almost 20 times the size of Great Britain) lies in the northern part of South America, between the Andes Mountains to the west, the high plateau of the Guyanas to the north, and the Mato Grosso plateau of Brazil to the south.

The Amazon River begins high in the mountains at over 15,000 feet (4,800 m). It is about 4,000 miles (7,000 km) long. With hundreds of tributaries, it forms the largest water reserve on earth. More than 250,000 cubic yards (200,000 cu m) of water flow out of its mouth

per second, sending fresh water 40 miles (64 km) out to sea. Floods occur from November to April.

Covering one-half or so of the South American continent, the Amazon basin is shared between Bolivia, Brazil, Columbia, Ecuador, Peru, and Venezuela.

The tropical forest

Lying on the Equator, the Amazon basin is always very warm. It is also very wet, with an average of more than 100 inches (254 cm) of rain each year. Because of this hot and wet climate, most of the area is covered by thick jungle with many different plants. A variety of animals live here—monkeys, meat-eating jaguars, and many reptiles, some of them poisonous.

The latex is smoked, then spun into a thread around a wooden stick to form a ball. Some 60,000 *seringueiros* (rubber tappers) still work in this way.

From left to right: Waura, Karajá, and Shuar peoples.

The Shuar people were known as the *Jivaro* for a long time. The invading Spanish had misheard and mispronounced the word *Shuar* which, like *Yanomami,* means men.

THE INDIGENOUS PEOPLES

Suya tribesman

A map of some of the Amazon tribes

Nambikwara tribesman

It is estimated that twelve to fifteen million Amerindians (indigenous peoples) lived in the Amazon basin when Europeans began to arrive in about 1500. Although the Amazon forest proved an obstacle for early explorers and colonizers, outside influences have caused the traditional Amerindian way of life to nearly vanish.

Apart from the largest tribes, most tribes now consist of just a few hundred, or even just a few dozen, people. Some of the Amerindian tribes include the Yanomami (about 20,000 people), the Siona (about

VENEZUELA

GUYANA

COLOMBIA

Orinoco

Arawak

SURINAM

FRENCH GUYANA

Guajibo

Yanomami
Xiriana

Apalai
Warikiana

Palikur

Cofan

Kobéwa
Tukano
Wanano

Karifuna

ECUADOR

Waorani

Amazon

Turiwàra
Tembé

Shuar

Jurunà
Arawete

Karajá

PERU

Apurana

Arara

Tapayuna
Kawahib   Tupi

Kayabi

Bororo
Paresi

Kampa

Urupa

Guaripuna
Cintas Largas

B R A Z I L

BOLIVIA

The Amazon peoples have always been aware of the fragility of their environment and food sources. They never kill more game, pick more plants, or cut down more trees than they need.

650), the Cofan (about 600), the Secoya (about 600), the Huaorami (about 1,000), the Eastern-Quechuas (about 60,000), and the Shuar (about 20,000). Known as the Jivaro, the Shuar were for a long time the best-known Amazonian tribe. They are fierce warriors and headhunters who fought back against the 16th-century Spanish conquistadores. They cut off their victims' heads, shrinking them to the size of a fist. A warrior's bravery was measured by the number of such skulls he owned.

Hunting and fishing

The peoples of the Amazon live mainly by hunting and fishing. They also gather fruit and nuts in the forest and clear patches of land to grow vegetables. Once it is cleared of trees, the forest soil is poor and any nutrients are soon washed away by heavy rain. Without fertilizer to feed the soil, the people are forced to move regularly in order to find a fresh patch of land. Men clear the forest, but it is women who sow and harvest the vegetables, such as manioc (a potato-like tuber), corn,

Xicrin child

pumpkins, beans, as well as tobacco and plantains. They do not breed pack animals to carry heavy loads for them. Most Amazon peoples practice shifting cultivation, although some rely on hunting and gathering in the forest.

The inventors of agriculture

Some scholars believe that the Amazon peoples were the first to develop agriculture in South America. These early farmers were tribespeople living by the major rivers where flooding enriched the soil with silt. Forced to move from the forest after a change in the climate, they probably climbed the Andes, following rivers to their source. They brought a knowledge of farming, and the first seeds, to the Pacific coast area stretching from northern Peru through most of Ecuador.

Yanomami men wear thin strings around their hips. Women wear small cotton skirts.

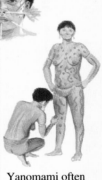
Yanomami often paint their body and face.

Below: warriors practice their skills on a stuffed dummy.

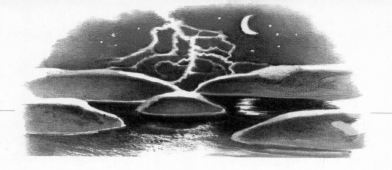

BELIEFS

Animal spirits are thought to look like the animal itself, but much bigger.

The Kamayurá believe the first people were born from trees. They hold a feast to celebrate this event, and play the long flutes shown below.

Spirits

The Amazonian people's believe that supernatural beings with vast power rule the world and influence events, acting directly on people's lives. These invisible creatures, or spirits, are the moving force behind every living being and every natural phenomenon. So, wind, thunder, the night, rivers—even illnesses—are displays of these forces.

There are spirits on every path in the forest and in every river and every vegetable patch. The whole world is sacred, and there are no barriers between the visible world and invisible forces. By cutting down a plant, for example, the spirit that protects it could be wounded. It is important, therefore, always to ask for the spirit's blessing.

The Vulture spirit, Fish spirit, Boar spirit, and so on are the masters or ancestors of those animals and control their existence on earth. Their good will must be obtained before going hunting.

Furthermore, each human being has a double in the animal world to whom they are joined until their death. If someone is ill, it could mean that their double is ill. This sort of belief is very common among the Amazonians. Some tribes believe they are descended from an animal. But not the Yanomami, who call themselves "children of the Moon." The moon, like the sun and the stars, is also a spirit.

Souls

Each person also has a spirit, or soul, which is different from their double. Some tribes believe every person has many souls, some of which they gain during their lifetime.

The Harakmbut, who live in southeast Peru, believe they each have two souls: a river soul and a forest soul. When they die, each soul enters into a small animal before joining the *serowe,* the underground river that is their paradise.

According to the Caribs, every person has five souls, each one a different color ranging from black to invisible.

The Shuar believe that they have only one soul, which mixes with their blood while they are alive. When they die, the soul moves to the house of the spirits, which is like the home of their birth. By taking hallucinogenic powder, someone may see the spirit of a long-dead Shuar who will give them another soul.

According to the Guarani, each person has two souls: one is vegetable, and the other is animal and gives the person their character.

The shaman

Although they are surrounded by spirits, the tribespeople can only communicate with them through the shaman. By taking hallucinogenic potions made from various forest plants, the shaman travels to the spirit world. He is given advice on subjects such as when to go hunting and is told what the future holds in store. The shaman is also a medicine man and understands the healing properties of plants. The spirits can tell him the cause of an illness and show him how to cure it. Amazon peoples believe spells cast by enemy shamans are the cause of most illnesses or violent deaths. The shaman calls on his *hékuras,* the spirits of the rocks, and unleashes dangerous animals, such as poisonous snakes, against his enemy.

A supreme god

Some Amazonian tribes—very few—believe in a supreme being, a god who created the world, usually represented by the sun.

The Yanomami creator god is called *Omame*. It is he who laid down the rules by which the Yanomami tribes live. Many different stories are told about the creation, and it is difficult to know exactly what *Omame* stands for.

Each community has its own shaman to protect it from any enemies.

When there has been a plentiful harvest or a good hunt, the Yanomami celebrate with a dish of plantain mash. They dress in leaves and feathers and paint their bodies. When the warriors set off for war, they paint their bodies black to symbolize strength and aggression.

At the top of the page is a picture drawn by a Yanomami shaman representing his journey to the spirit world. The spirits he called up are shown in pink and purple. The straight lines mark the path he took.

The instrument shown above is a bullroarer. It is whirled round on a string to produce an eerie sound. The peoples of the Amazon consider it a sacred instrument and a messenger of the spirits.

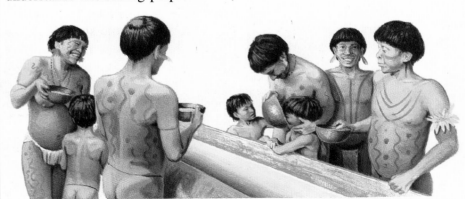

RITES

The Makuna people celebrate the meeting of humans and nature in death by asking for the blessing of the dead person's spirit. The rite takes place in the house of spirits, which is always elaborately decorated.

The shaman does not adore the spirits. He takes advantage of their special knowledge because, according to native beliefs, their world is the real world, while ours is just a reflection. There is no organized worship, but various rituals mark the important steps in life.

Initiation rites

When girls are old enough to get married, they have to undergo a cruel test. They are locked up for weeks, even months, in a corner of the hut and may only go out at night, with their heads covered. Some tribes mark this rite of passage by pulling out tufts of the girl's hair.

Among the Wayana people on the Upper Maroni River (between Surinam and French Guyana), boys and girls dance for a day and a night, before undergoing the trial of the *maraqué*. Wasps and ants are put into a basket: the master of ceremonies passes this over the dancers' naked bodies. The insect bites are itchy and uncomfortable, but no one is allowed to show pain.

Death rites

There are many different rites surrounding death. Until a short time ago, many tribes still left their dead out to dry, and later pounded the mummy into a powder that they dissolved in beer.

The Shuar bury their dead in a corner of their home, to protect them from the cold nights. Other tribes destroy all the dead person's possessions, fearing that they will come back to haunt those who use their belongings.

During the ceremonies that mark a child's passage into adulthood, some tribes wear painted masks depicting animals or fantastical creatures.

To make sure the harvest is good, Kaiapó shamans undertake a fertility rite. Dressed in reeds from head to toe, they perform a long and complex dance.

SAVE THE YANOMAMI

The Waorani in Ecuador are in the same danger as the Yanomami. Their traditional lands are being devastated by the oil industry.

Gold teeth are a sure sign that a *garimpeiro,* or miner, has struck lucky!

On the far right, miners in an open-cast gold mine carry sacks of mud—and perhaps gold.

Mercury is used to separate gold from sand. It is poisonous both to those who use it and to the environment.

Today, there are only a million native peoples left in the Amazon forest.

The first Europeans who came to the Americas knew of the existence of such tribespeople, but the density of the forest, and its great size, meant that contact was sporadic until this century.

The destruction of a way of life

Toward the end of the last century, the growth of the automobile industry led to a huge demand for rubber to make tires. This caused the first invasion of the forest.

Then, in the 1960s, prospectors found that the Amazon was rich in mineral deposits: iron, petroleum, tin, gold, and diamonds. Large areas of the forest were cleared in order to exploit them. At the same time, trees were felled to make way for huge plantations and industrial cattle stations. The northern perimeter highway was bulldozed through part of the forest.

The arrival of miners brought many diseases, including malaria, which had a terrible effect on the indigenous population, who had no natural resistance to these diseases.

The future of the Yanomami

The Yanomami in Brazil number about 7,500 and occupy an area of 23.2 million acres. In May 1992, this area was officially made a Yanomami reserve. In Venezuela, the Yanomami tribal lands were declared a biosphere reserve in 1991. But it is difficult to protect the boundaries of these areas, and mining companies as well as the military are keen to have access.

The death toll due to the diseases brought by miners and other outsiders is rising.

Meanwhile, the rivers, their flora and fauna, are being polluted with the mercury used in refining minerals. Basic foods that the tribespeople have relied on for thousands of years are now threatened.

Despite measures to protect them, the Yanomami are in danger of complete extinction.

In 1993, a team of *garimpeiros* killed sixteen Yanomami. The Brazilian authorities are investigating the case. Despite all the obstacles, the Yanomami are determined to survive and are beginning to organize themselves to stand up to pressures from outside.